Rodeo Surprise

The two singers burst through the exit. They were shocked to discover that they had run out into the middle of the rodeo arena.

The crowd clapped and shouted when they appeared.

Donnie and Jonathan didn't know what was going on. But they soon found out.

The announcer on the loudspeaker said, "And our next act is the Diddle Brothers, the best rodeo clowns west of Fresno!"

The crowd cheered again. Donnie and Jonathan waved back to them.

"What do we do now?" asked Jonathan, as he tightened the ribbon on his blue bonnet.

"Sing a few bars of 'Hangin' Tough'?"

"I don't think that's what these people are waiting for."

"Then what do you suggest?"

"I suggest we get away from that bull over there."

Donnie swung around. A huge black bull was charging across the arena, heading straight for them!

The Novels

NEW KIDS ON THE BLOCK

On Stage

Seth McEvoy and Laure Smith

AN ARCHWAY PAPERBACK
Published by POCKET BOOKS

New York   London   Toronto   Sydney   Tokyo   Singapore

AN ARCHWAY PAPERBACK *Original*

An Archway Paperback published by
POCKET BOOKS, a division of Simon & Schuster Inc.
1230 Avenue of the Americas, New York, NY 10020

Text and cover art copyright © 1991 by Big Step Productions, Inc.
Song titles and lyrics copyright © 1991 by Maurice Starr
Music, Inc., used by permission of Maurice Starr.

Packaged by March Tenth, Inc.

Winterland
productions
ROCK EXPRESS ®

ISBN: 0-671-73940-9

First Archway Paperback printing July 1991

10 9 8 7 6 5 4 3 2 1

Cover art by Franco Accornero

Printed in the U.S.A.

IL 6+

On Stage

Chapter

1

THE NEW KIDS' TOUR BUS was parked behind the Red Rock Mall in Red Rock, California. The five singers were waiting in the bus for the mall to open at ten o'clock that morning. Donnie, Danny, Jordan, and Joe were in the back playing video games with Biscuit, their bodyguard.

Jonathan Knight sat in the front seat glancing at his watch every two minutes. Finally it was ten o'clock and he yelled to the others, "It's time to go to the mall." Then he bolted out of his seat and was the first one out the door.

He quickly hurried across the nearly

deserted parking lot. Donnie Wahlberg rushed out of the bus and called out to Jonathan, but Jonathan didn't answer. He kept right on going. The last thing he wanted to do was talk to Donnie. He was really mad at him.

Donnie was determined to straighten things out with Jonathan. He ran up beside him. "I know you're angry at me about the shoes, Jonathan, but I promise I won't do it again."

"I hope not. Do you realize that you ruined my favorite pair of high-top basketball sneakers?"

"I'm sorry," said Donnie. "I didn't mean to drop a whole pepperoni pizza on them. It was an accident."

Jonathan suddenly stopped and spun around. "What do you mean, it was an accident? You did it on purpose."

"No, I didn't," Donnie said. "I accidently tripped and the pizza pie just flew out of my hand. I'm *really* sorry."

Jonathan stuffed his hands into his pockets as Biscuit and the other New Kids came up beside him.

Donnie put his hand on Jonathan's shoulder. "Please don't be mad at me. I'll buy you a brand-new pair. Then we'll have a great time at the Frontier Festival this afternoon. Okay?"

Jonathan looked over at the mall as he thought about what Donnie had said.

"Don't be mad at Donnie," Jordan Knight told his brother. "Let's forget about it and go inside."

"I'm going on ahead," said Danny Wood. "I have a few things I need to buy at the five-and-dime."

"I'll go with you," Joe McIntyre replied. "We'll meet you guys in the shoe store in half an hour."

Just as he turned to leave, Biscuit grabbed Joe by the arm. The big, muscular man easily stopped him dead in his tracks. "Hey, wait a minute, Joe. Dick ordered me to keep you boys all together. Remember what he told you about that rumor. He heard that a local radio station may be running a contest offering prizes to anyone who can bring back a personal souvenir from the New Kids on the Block. If it's true, I'll need to keep a close watch on you guys."

"Don't worry about us," Joe replied. "We'll be careful."

"I know," said Biscuit. "But Dick gave me strict orders. He's concerned about the rumor. He doesn't want any of you wandering off and getting into trouble."

"Who, us?" asked Danny. "We'd never do that."

Biscuit laughed out loud. "What about that time in Phoenix when you took off after your concert? You disappeared for hours. Dick and I looked everywhere for you."

"We were hungry," Donnie explained. "We just went out to get a few hamburgers."

"Yeah, but then you ran into some old friends from Boston," said Biscuit. "And you went horseback riding someplace in the middle of the night."

"That was great!" Jordan exclaimed. "Our friends took us to a riding stable that was open twenty-four hours. We rode all over this huge park in the moonlight. It was chillin'. I even saw a real roadrunner."

"You did not," Danny replied. "It was an old tin can that my horse had kicked across the ground."

"No way," Jordan protested. "It was a roadrunner. I'm sure of it. It had long feathers in its tail, just like the cartoon character."

"You're crazy," Danny replied.

Jordan made a face at Danny.

Joe put his arms around both of them. "Cool down, guys. Maybe it was a road-runner, maybe it wasn't. It doesn't really matter that much, does it?"

Jordan shrugged his shoulders. "I guess not."

"Okay, then," said Joe. "Let's go get Jonathan some new basketball shoes."

Jonathan agreed. Then they all walked over to the back entrance of the Red Rock Mall.

When they went inside, Biscuit was relieved to discover that there weren't very many customers there yet. It was his job to make sure the New Kids weren't mobbed by fans, so he always felt better when there weren't very many people around.

Most of the New Kids' fans were friendly and kind. But once in a while the fans would get so excited to see their favorite singers that they'd go wild. The New Kids loved to meet their admirers, except when they tore at their clothes and pulled their hair. That's when they needed Biscuit.

On the way to the shoe store, the five

singers and their bodyguard stopped at a snack counter. They had already had breakfast on the bus earlier but, as usual, found themselves hungry again. Jonathan and Jordan each ordered an egg-muffin sandwich, while Danny, Biscuit, and Joe had pancakes and sausage. Donnie usually ate three times as much as everyone else, but this morning he didn't order anything.

Danny was surprised when his old friend said he wasn't hungry. For as long as he'd known him, Donnie would eat every chance he could get. He and Donnie had been friends since elementary school. They'd done everything together. They were as close as brothers. So Danny knew there must be something wrong if Donnie passed up an opportunity to eat.

When the food arrived, he said to Donnie, "These pancakes are great. You should try some."

"No, thanks," Donnie replied without even looking over at them. He just stared off into space.

Joe also noticed that Donnie didn't seem to be himself. He thought that

Donnie was being awfully quiet. He was usually the life of the party, laughing and joking and teasing everyone all the time. But not now.

Joe told Donnie that he was going to get another carton of orange juice, and he asked if Donnie wanted one, too. When he didn't answer, Joe wasn't sure what to do. He was worried about his friend. He'd never seen Donnie turn down food before.

When Jordan finished his sandwich, he began tapping his straw on the edge of the table, thumping out the beat of a new song. He was so lost in his own thoughts that he wasn't aware of anything around him.

But Jonathan was; he was the oldest and he kept an eye on everyone else in the group. He quickly realized that something was wrong with Donnie. He was afraid that he had hurt Donnie's feelings when he had gotten mad at him about the basketball shoes. "Donnie," said Jonathan, "are you all right?"

Donnie stared at the stores on the other side of the mall. Finally he answered, "Yeah, sure, I'm fine."

"The food here is great," Jonathan told him. "Why don't I get you a couple of orders of scrambled eggs?"

Donnie shook his head. "No, thanks. I'm not hungry."

Danny and Joe looked at each other. They were more worried than before. Biscuit was, too.

Jonathan decided that he had to find out what was wrong right away. "Come over here for a second," he said, motioning Donnie to a nearby table. "I've got to talk to you."

Donnie looked puzzled as they both sat down. "What's going on?"

"That's what I want to ask you," Jonathan replied. "You seem kind of down. I was wondering if you were feeling all right."

"Like I said before, I'm fine."

"Then how come you aren't eating anything? Are you mad at me?"

"Why would I be mad at you?"

"Because of what happened with my shoes. I really gave you a tough time about that."

"You had a good reason to be angry. Those were your favorite shoes and I ruined them. You had every right to be

8

mad at me. It was a stupid thing to do. I'm really sorry about it."

"I know," Jonathan replied. "But it was just an accident. I shouldn't have been so hard on you."

Donnie absentmindedly fingered the napkin holder on the table. "I've been thinking," he said. "I realized that your shoes were ruined because I had to have a pizza. Pigging out has gotten me into trouble more than once. From now on, I'm not going to eat so much."

Jonathan was startled. "But—" he began. Donnie cut him off.

"Don't try and change my mind," he insisted. "My mind is made up. I don't want to hear another word about it."

Even though Donnie told him not to, Jonathan felt he had to try and help him. He didn't think it was a good idea to take such drastic action, at least for Donnie. He knew how determined Donnie could be when he decided to do something. There was no holding him back. He had a will of iron. On the other hand, Donnie also had an amazing appetite. Jonathan felt really bad about Donnie's decision. He worried that it was his fault. He feared that he had been too harsh with him. "I don't think you should do this because of me."

Donnie pushed his chair back from the table. "Like I said before, my mind is made up."

"But—" Jonathan started to protest.

"I told you," Donnie said, cutting him off again. "I don't want to hear another word about it. Now let's go buy you a new pair of shoes."

Donnie walked back over to the other table and everyone got up to leave, but Jonathan sat there for a few more seconds. He was really worried about Donnie. He didn't know what to do. Finally he decided that all he could do was keep a close watch on him to make sure he was going to be all right.

When Jonathan joined the others, Danny asked, "What happened?"

"I'll tell you later."

Biscuit and the five singers went across to the other side of the mall. They stopped at a store where Danny and Joe bought shaving cream and new razors. Jordan picked up the latest issue of *Electronic Keyboard* magazine. Biscuit grabbed up an armload of pretzels, potato chips, and cheese popcorn.

"Hey, Donnie, I got two bags of your favorite barbecue chips," said the bodyguard.

"I won't be eating them anymore," he answered. "Give them to someone else."

Biscuit couldn't believe his ears. Neither could Danny and Joe.

"Did he say what I thought he said?" asked Danny.

"I think so," Biscuit replied.

"You heard right," Donnie told him. "I've given up my old ways; it's time for a new me. From now on, I'm only going to eat as much as the rest of you do."

Danny was shocked. "Do you mean to tell me that we've seen the last of Donnie the human garbage can?"

"That's right," he answered. "If you eat two hot dogs for lunch, then that's all I'm having."

"But you always eat at least five or six," said Joe.

"Not anymore," Donnie replied.

Chapter

2

THE NEW KIDS spotted the shoe store and Biscuit led them all inside. They rushed over to the huge display of running shoes lined up along the wall. Jonathan carefully searched through the dozens of different styles, looking for the same kind as he had before. Danny and Joe checked out the store displays while Jordan sat down on one of the chairs and started to read his keyboard magazine.

Donnie grabbed a pair of lime-green sneakers. "I've been wanting a pair of shoes like these for years."

A young male salesclerk came over to

Donnie. "Would you like to try on a pair of those?" he asked.

"Yeah!" Donnie replied.

The clerk quickly measured Donnie's foot; then he hurried off to the stockroom.

"Hey, Jonathan," said Donnie. "Did you find your shoes yet?"

"No," he answered. "I don't see them anywhere."

"Which ones are you looking for?" asked the clerk as he came out carrying a white box.

Jonathan described them, and the clerk told him that that style had been discontinued.

Donnie saw that Jonathan was disappointed, so he said, "Why don't you try something new, like these?" He held up one of the bright green shoes.

Jonathan made a face. "No, thanks. I'll pick out something else."

The clerk pulled the green tennis shoes out of the box and Donnie's eyes lit up. "Oh, good, you've got them in my size."

The clerk slipped them on. "Are you guys going to the Red Rock Frontier Festival?"

"Definitely," Donnie replied. "We heard it's slammin'."

"You've never gone to it before?"

"No, we haven't."

"You'll love it. It's great. I've been going every year for as long as I can remember. My favorite part is the Fort Apache Funhouse. It's really scary. You should check it out."

"We will," Donnie said. He stood up to test his shoes. "These are perfect. I'll take them. What about you, Jonathan? Have you found something yet?"

"Yeah. I think I'll get a pair of these blue-and-white high tops."

"I'll go check and see if we have them in your size," said the clerk.

Soon he returned with a box under his arm. Jonathan put on the shoes and laced them up the way he liked them. Then he slowly walked across the floor, carefully examining how they fit.

"I'll take them," he announced.

"Will that be all?" inquired the clerk. "Is there anything else you need?"

Jonathan shook his head.

"Will that be cash or charge?"

"Cash," Donnie replied. "These are on me."

"Thanks, Donnie," said Jonathan. "I appreciate it."

Donnie called out to Biscuit and the other New Kids. "We're almost done; are you guys getting anything?"

"No," they all answered.

"We're ready to go," said Danny.

The clerk rang up the order and handed Donnie his bag. Then everyone left the store and went back out into the mall.

As they crossed over to the stores on the other side, Joe pointed to someone up ahead. "Isn't that Hank Barclay from our lighting crew?"

"I think so," said Danny. "I know his family lives here in Red Rock, and he's the only person in the world with curly red hair like that."

"The girl that's with him has the same color hair," said Joe. "Maybe that's his sister, Susannah. Hank told me about her last night after the concert. He said she was really nice and smart, too!"

"Well, that sounds like my kind of girl," Donnie said. "Let's go meet her."

Donnie darted in front of the others and called out to Hank. The lighting man smiled when he turned around and saw the New Kids.

"Hi, guys," Hank said with a wave. "What are you doing out here at the mall? I thought you were supposed to be at the Frontier Festival today."

"We're going over there in a few minutes," said Donnie. "But we had to pick up a few things first."

Joe nudged Hank in the arm. Then he leaned over and asked, "Is that your sister?"

Hank nodded. "Let me introduce you to my little sister. This is Susannah. She's a big fan of yours."

Joe stepped up to shake her hand. "It's nice to finally meet you. Hank has told me lots of good things about you."

Susannah looked down shyly. She tried not to blush, but her cheeks quickly turned as red as her hair. "Hank talks about you New Kids all of the time. He says you have a lot of fun on tour."

"Oh, yeah," said Donnie, leaning forward and pushing Joe to the side. "Did he tell you that I'm the best dancer in the group?"

"Well . . . ah . . . ," she stammered, not sure what to say.

Joe shoved Donnie back. "Don't let him make you nervous."

Susannah smiled at Joe. "I won't."

Jonathan, Jordan, Danny, and Biscuit each said hello. Susannah told the singers how much she liked their music.

"What's your favorite song?" Donnie asked.

"Come on, Wahlberg," Joe protested. "Quit putting her on the spot."

"That question is easy to answer," she replied. "My favorite song is 'Please Don't Go, Girl.'"

"That's *my* song!" Joe beamed proudly.

"I like it a lot," said Susannah. "My friends and I sing it together every day on our way to school."

"I'd like to hear that sometime," said Joe. "Maybe you and your friends could come hear us and come backstage after our show tonight." Joe reached into his pocket and pulled out concert tickets and backstage passes. He offered them to Susannah.

"We already have our tickets," she said.

"Then take these backstage passes so you can come visit us after the show."

"Thanks a lot," Susannah replied.

All of a sudden, someone let out a

piercing scream. The group whirled around to see what was wrong. They were shocked to discover a huge crowd of girls running straight at them.

"Let's get moving," yelled Biscuit. He pointed to the right and told everyone to head for the side exit.

Hank and Susannah dashed away from the fans right alongside them. Just before they reached the side door, another group of screaming fans swarmed in from outside.

"They're coming at us from all directions," shouted Danny.

"We're trapped," cried Joe.

"No, you're not," said Susannah. "Follow me." She raced over to the pizza parlor across the hallway. "I used to work here. We can sneak out their back door."

The fans were moving in as she led everyone inside. "Hey, Ronald," she yelled. "Unlock the back door. We're coming through."

"What?" said Ronald.

"There's no time to explain," she shouted. "Please unlock the door, then whip up a few dozen extra pizzas, because you'll be getting a lot of customers real soon!"

Ronald quickly pulled out his keys and rushed to the rear entrance. The New Kids followed him through the storage room to the back door. The fans were pouring inside the pizza parlor as the five singers ran outside.

"Thanks a lot," Susannah said to Ronald. "Just tell all those girls inside that the New Kids stopped by. You'll sell a million slices of pizza."

"I'll do that!" he answered as they ran out into the parking lot.

The band's bus was parked nearby; they all raced toward it as fast as they could. When they flew inside, Biscuit yelled to the bus driver, "Start the engine. We've got to get out of here!"

Chapter

3

THE NEW KIDS' TOUR BUS pulled out of the mall parking lot and onto the main boulevard. Hank and Susannah sat down next to Joe and Donnie.

"That sure was close," exclaimed Danny, dropping into his seat.

"You know it!" Jordan replied.

"You pulled us out of a tight spot," Joe told Susannah. "Thanks a lot. Ducking into that pizza place was a great move."

"I told you she was smart," said Hank.

Susannah lowered her head and looked away, embarrassed. She was glad the New Kids liked how she had helped them, but she was a little uncomfortable that everyone was talking about her.

"What's going on out here?" asked the New Kids' manager, Dick Scott, as he came out from a room in the back of the bus.

Jonathan told him what had happened at the mall. Dick was pleased to hear that Susannah had helped them escape. But he was worried that the New Kids might not be so lucky the next time.

"I hope you boys will be more careful at the Frontier Festival this afternoon," he said. "There will be thousands of people there. Remember what I said about that rumor I heard. If a local radio station really does have a contest to see who can bring in personal New Kids' souvenirs, things could get crazy if anyone recognizes you."

"Don't worry about us," said Jonathan. "We'll be dressed up in western clothes like everyone else. No one will know who we are."

"Hey, Biscuit," yelled Donnie. "Where did you put those cowboy hats we bought yesterday?"

"They're in the cupboard under Joe's bunk," he replied.

Donnie rushed over and threw open the small doors. He pulled out the bag of hats and dug around inside until he found the one he was looking for. "Here it is." He held up a bright red cowboy hat.

Donnie pulled on the oversized hat and reached out his arms. "How do you like it?"

"It's perfect!" Danny replied. "It's loud and obnoxious, just like you are."

Donnie made a face at Danny. "You know, Danny, if you don't watch what you say, one of these days somebody is going to stuff a sock in your mouth."

Joe laughed. Then he jumped up to get one of the cowboy hats. He lifted a white one out of the bag and slid it on.

Jonathan and Jordan each put on their black ones. Danny's hat was light tan and had a row of feathers around the band.

"Are the cowboy shirts we bought in this cupboard, too?" Donnie asked Biscuit.

The bodyguard nodded. "That's where I put them."

23

Donnie looked puzzled as he felt around inside. "There's nothing else in here. It's completely empty."

"Oh, I forgot to tell you," said Jonathan. "I ironed all of our shirts and hung them in the closet."

"When did you do that?" asked Donnie.

"At three o'clock in the morning. Last night I couldn't sleep, so I got up and did a few things around here. I cleaned out the refrigerator and alphabetized all of the video games. Then I decided to iron a few things."

"You didn't iron my socks again, did you?" asked Jordan. "I hate it when you do that."

"No, I didn't iron your socks. But I did do your T-shirts."

"Gee, thanks," Jordan said sarcastically.

Donnie opened the closet and took out the shirts. He held them up for Dick to see. "If we wear these with our jeans and the cowboy hats, no one will know who we are."

Dick looked doubtful.

"I've got some bandannas we could wear around our necks," said Danny.

"Then we could pull them up over our faces if anyone suspects it's us."

"Maybe if you do that, you won't be recognized," said Dick. "But I have to admit that I'm still a little nervous about letting you guys go out into a big crowd like that. Fans may be looking for you everywhere."

"We'll be just fine," Joe told him.

"You'd better be careful," Dick warned. "Because next time you get mobbed, you won't have Susannah to help you out."

"Maybe we will," Joe replied. He then leaned over and whispered into her ear. "Would you like to go to the Frontier Festival with us today?"

"Yes," Susannah answered. "I'd love to."

Joe joyfully clapped his hands together. "Great!" he cheered. "Susannah said she'll go with us to the festival."

"I'm glad to hear it," said Dick. "Maybe she can keep you guys out of trouble."

"I'll try," Susannah said.

"You can count on her," said Hank. "She may seem shy, but she can handle anything."

25

Dick suddenly snapped his fingers. "Oh, that reminds me. Hank, I need to talk to you about a lighting problem that just came up."

"Sure thing," Hank replied.

He and Dick sat down together, and Donnie and Danny put on their western shirts. Jonathan and Jordan both pulled cans of soda out of the refrigerator, while Joe and Susannah talked quietly together.

"You'll love the Frontier Festival," she told Joe. "It's held at Laredo Village. There are tons of cool things to do there. They have an old western town and a huge carnival with lots of unusual rides. I like the rodeo the best."

"When I was little, I wanted to be a cowboy," said Joe. "I used to watch westerns on TV. I liked this show called 'The Cactus Kid.' It was about an orphan boy who made friends with an Indian scout. They went everywhere together and had all kinds of adventures. I think it would be chillin' to be able to ride a horse in the mountains."

"It is," Susannah replied. "My uncle has a stable up near Lake Tahoe. We go there every summer and ride through the trails. It's one of my favorite places in the whole world."

"I'd love to go there." Then, as he glanced out the window, he exclaimed, "Look at that crowd out there. I wonder what's going on."

Susannah leaned over to get a better look. She accidentally brushed up against Joe's shoulder and quickly pulled away.

"What's wrong?" he asked.

"Oh . . . ah . . . nothing." Susannah peered out the window again. "Those people are all going to the Wild West Revue. It's a musical show about the old West."

"Is it good?" Joe asked.

"Yeah. It's a lot of fun."

"Maybe we could go see it sometime." Joe suggested.

"I know the assistant manager of the theater," Susannah replied. "I'll ask him if he can get us six good tickets."

"No, not six," said Joe. "Just two. One for you and one for me."

Susannah was surprised. She had never expected that Joe would ask her out on a date. She'd never even dared hope it would happen. But she was

27

thrilled that it had. "You really want me to get just two tickets?"

"If that's okay with you," Joe asked nervously.

"Oh, sure," she told him. "I'd like to go to the Wild West Revue with you."

"Good," he said with a sigh of relief. At first he'd been afraid that Susannah didn't want to be with him, but now that she had said yes, he could hardly wait.

Joe and Susannah talked quietly together while the rest of the New Kids finished changing their clothes. Dick Scott and Hank were busy looking over a large map of the theater where the concert would be held that evening.

"Hey, Joe," yelled Jonathan. "You had better hurry up and get dressed. Biscuit told me that we'll be arriving at the festival any minute."

"Okay," he answered. "I'll be there right away." Joe turned to Susannah and said, "I have to change. Is there anything I can get for you? A soda? Or some potato chips?"

"No, thanks," she replied. "I'm fine."

"How about a magazine?" asked Joe. "We've got lots of them around here someplace. Now, where did they go?"

Joe searched under the seats and through the overhead racks.

"Come on, Joe!" yelled Jonathan.

"Just a second," he shouted back. "I can't find the magazines."

"I put them in a box behind the driver's seat," he answered.

"It figures," said Joe, reaching into the box. "If you can't find something, just ask Jonathan. He probably put it away when you weren't looking. He's a real neatnik."

Susannah laughed and Joe handed her two magazines. "Thanks," she said.

Joe went to the back of the bus and Jonathan tossed him his shirt. Donnie pushed his way past both of them. He was all dressed up in a blue-and-white check shirt, yellow bandanna, and his big red cowboy hat.

"I think I'll go keep Susannah company," he said.

"Oh, no, you're not!" Joe declared. "I'll be dressed in no time at all."

Joe pulled on his green-striped shirt as fast as he could. He grabbed up his white cowboy hat with one hand and struggled to snap up his buttons with the other. He rushed back to the front of the bus just as Donnie was sitting down next to Susannah.

"I think you're in my seat," he said to Donnie.

"There are plenty of other empty seats," Donnie replied. He pointed across the aisle. "You can sit over there."

"But I was sitting where you are," Joe insisted.

"Oh, come on, Joe, I haven't had a chance to talk to Susannah yet."

Joe thought fast, then said, "Donnie, Jordan is in the back eating a donut. He told me he didn't want the other half. Do you want it?"

Donnie leapt to his feet. He started for the back of the bus—then he froze in his tracks. "I almost forgot. I don't want to stuff myself anymore."

Donnie turned around to return to his seat, but before he could get there, Joe darted in front of him and quickly sat down next to Susannah.

Joe grinned up at Donnie.

"I bet you think you're smart, don't you, McIntyre?"

Joe didn't answer. He kept right on grinning.

Chapter

4

THE NEW KIDS' TOUR BUS pulled into Laredo Village. The old West amusement park was a huge tourist attraction on the edge of Red Rock. The park included an old frontier town, carnival rides, a rodeo arena, riding stables, and a ghost town.

Thousands of people came from all over the country to visit the park every year. But even more came during the big annual Frontier Festival. Everyone dressed up in western costumes and there were special activities each day. The New Kids were scheduled to perform at a big concert the first night.

When the bus came to a stop, the five singers jumped up and rushed to the door. They were excited that they had the afternoon off. They had been looking forward to the festival for a long time.

Donnie was the first one out of the bus. "Heigh-ho Silver, here I come," he shouted, throwing his hat up in the air.

Dick Scott climbed off the bus right behind him. "I hope you're going to keep that hat on, or else somebody might recognize you."

Donnie slid the red cowboy hat back into place. "Just call me Pecos Donnie, King of the Rio Grande."

Susannah and the other New Kids laughed.

Then Dick instructed Biscuit to keep close watch on them all. "Don't forget that you guys have an important concert at five o'clock," he said. "I hope that you have a great time today, but be sure to get to the theater on time."

"They'll be there," Biscuit promised. "I'll make sure of it."

Dick slapped him on the back. "Thanks," he told him. "Hank and I will be taking the bus back to the theater parking lot. You can call me there if you need anything. Oh, by the way, Jonathan, here are your passes to the festival. See you guys later!"

"Let's posse up and ride on out of here," Donnie announced.

"Wait a second," said Susannah. She turned around to her brother. "Hank, will you call Mom and tell her that I won't be home until after the concert tonight?"

"Sure thing," he answered.

Susannah waved good-bye and everyone headed off. Huge crowds of people were pouring into the park. Almost all of them wore colorful western costumes. A lot of people had on blue jeans and cowboy hats just like the New Kids. Some were dressed as Indians. Others wore black hats and ruffled shirts like the Spanish settlers. And two people came in a big gray horse costume.

When they reached the front gate, Jonathan handed the ticket seller the special passes that Dick Scott had given him. The young girl in the booth gave them each a map and a program guide.

She explained that their admission included most of the rides and attractions. Then she smiled and waved them on through.

"This is going to be total magic," Danny exclaimed as they went inside. "Look at all the people here."

"The place is packed," said Jonathan.

The main street of the frontier town was spread out in front of them. The old-fashioned buildings featured shops that sold food, gifts, and wild-West souvenirs. Over to the left, the New Kids could see the carnival rides rising high up into the air.

Joe stood in the middle of the busy street as he looked at his program guide. All of a sudden, a runaway toddler rushed up and grabbed him by the leg.

"I'm sorry," said the little boy's mother as she gently pulled him away.

"Don't worry about it," answered Joe. "I love kids." He patted the little boy on the head. "I'd like to have one just like you someday," he told him.

The mother beamed proudly. "Thanks for being so understanding."

"No problem," Joe replied. "Like I said, I'm crazy about kids."

"Then you'll make a good father," she told him.

"I hope I will, but not for a while," said Joe.

The woman put her baby safely back in his stroller and quickly disappeared into the sea of tourists.

"What should we do first?" asked Jordan.

"Let's go on some rides!" Danny declared.

Donnie rubbed his stomach and glanced around. "Is anybody hungry?"

"No, not me," replied Danny.

The others shook their heads no.

Jonathan pointed across the crowd. "There's a chili dog stand over there. We'll wait for you if you want to go get something."

"No," answered Donnie. "If no one else is having anything, then neither am I!"

Jonathan was worried that Donnie wasn't going to get enough to eat, so he said, "Well, maybe I am a little hungry. Why don't you go grab us some chili dogs and a couple of cans of soda?"

"Are you sure?" asked Donnie.

"You're not just saying that to make me eat, are you?"

Jonathan hesitated. "Well . . . ah . . . no. You know how much I like chili dogs. Let's get some."

"Okay. I'll be right back."

Jonathan was relieved when Donnie rushed off. He was glad that his friend hadn't pressed him to tell the truth and admit that he wasn't really hungry. And he was happy that his plan had worked, that he was able to get Donnie to eat.

Donnie quickly returned and handed Jonathan his food. Then Donnie wolfed down his chili dog in less than ten seconds.

Jonathan struggled to finish his, but he couldn't quite eat the last few bites. He hid the remaining piece in his hand and threw it away with his half-empty can of soda.

"Come on," Jordan urged. "Let's go check out the rides."

"I'm with ya'," Donnie replied. "How about you?" he asked Susannah. "Are you ready to go on some rides?"

Susannah nodded eagerly. "I'd love to."

"Since you've been here before," said Donnie, "you must know all of the good rides."

"Every one of them is great," she answered.

Donnie stepped closer to her. "But which one is your favorite?"

Joe glared at Donnie. He wished he would leave Susannah alone, because he wanted her all to himself. Joe feared that she might be more interested in Donnie. A lot of the fans liked Donnie the best. He was loads of fun.

Joe edged up closer to Susannah, but Donnie didn't pay any attention to him; he kept right on talking. Then suddenly Donnie started to sing:

> *"Oh, Susannah, won't you come*
>   *with me,*
> *On the triple-decker Ferris wheel,*
> *Where we'll see what we can see?"*

"Oh, no," groaned Danny. "That's the dumbest song I ever heard."

"I thought it was pretty good," said Donnie. "Maybe I'll become a country and western singer." He stretched out his arms, reared back his head, and sang out:

> *"I'm a singing cowboy,*
> *Riding the range,*
> *With my trusty horse, Rhubarb,*
> *Who's covered with mange."*

Before he could sing another note, Danny put his hand over Donnie's mouth. "You're a silent cowboy, now!"

Donnie pulled away. "You don't appreciate good music when you hear it."

"Sure I do," Danny replied. "But that wasn't it! Listen, I think I hear some good music up ahead."

"You're right," Jordan exclaimed. "Someone's playing our song."

"I hear it, too," said Jonathan. "It's 'The Right Stuff.' "

Joe pointed over to the Wagon Wheel Saloon. "It's coming from inside there."

"Let's go check it out," Donnie replied.

He and the others scurried across the crowded street and up onto the wooden plank sidewalk. Donnie pushed open the swinging front doors.

They were all surprised when they discovered five dancers onstage in old-fashioned long dresses with aprons and sunbonnets. The teenage girls were singing along with a jukebox that was playing the New Kids' song "The Right Stuff." The roomful of customers watched as they danced together in a line and belted out the chorus:

"Oh, oh, oh, oh, oh . . . the right stuff!"

When the last note was played, the crowd broke into thunderous applause. The girls bowed and ran offstage to take up their other jobs as waitresses. One of the girls rushed behind the bar, where snacks and sodas were for sale.

Danny pulled his tan cowboy hat down over his eyes and stepped up to the counter. He ordered a can of apple juice. When the waitress brought it to him at the table, he said, "That was a pretty good performance."

"Thanks," the girl replied with a big, happy grin. "We do that song all the time. The customers love it."

"What other songs do you perform here?" asked Donnie.

"Oh, lots of them. We can sing anything on the jukebox. But 'The Right Stuff' is the most popular."

"How often do you do these performances?" asked Jordan.

"Every half hour. Or sometimes we do them more often if the customers want us to."

"You do a nice job," said Jordan. "Almost as good as the New Kids themselves."

"No way!" the girl protested. "The New Kids are the best. We'll never be as good as they are."

Donnie leaned forward. "I don't know about that," he said. "You girls were slick. Are any of you planning on going into show biz?"

"Oh, no! We just do this for fun. I want to be a veterinarian someday."

"That's great," said Jonathan. "I love animals."

"Really?" the girl replied.

"Oh, yeah. If I wasn't a—" Jonathan suddenly stopped short. He had almost told the girl who he was. Fortunately his big black cowboy hat hid his true identity. "That's right, I love animals," he told her, quickly covering his tracks. "I've had dozens of pets."

"Me, too," said the waitress. "I've got two dogs, three cats, an old horse, and a one-legged pigeon."

"A one-legged pigeon?" Jonathan exclaimed. "What happened to him?"

"It's a her. I found her lying by the side of the road on my way home from school one day. I think she had been hit by a car. I took her to my house and nursed her back to health. Now she's as good as new and she hops all over the place."

Danny threw away his empty juice can. "Are you guys about ready to hit the rides?"

"Sure," Donnie exclaimed. "Lead the way."

"It was nice talking to you," Jonathan told the waitress.

"You did a super job singing to that New Kids song," said Jordan.

"That's because we're big fans of theirs," she replied.

"Will you be at their concert tonight?" asked Jonathan.

"Absolutely. I can hardly wait. I'm dying to go."

41

"Maybe we'll see you there," said Jonathan.

"You guys are New Kids' fans?" she asked.

Jonathan nodded. "They're our favorite group."

"Well, then, I'll be looking for you at the concert," the girl told him.

"I'll be wearing a big white Red Sox baseball shirt," he said.

"I'll watch out for it," she replied.

"Good," Jonathan answered. Then he waved good-bye and left with the others.

Danny rushed on ahead of everyone. He was anxious to get to the rides. He darted through the crowd so fast the rest had trouble keeping up.

This made Biscuit nervous. He didn't want to lose sight of Danny. "Hey, Danny, wait for us," the bodyguard yelled.

"I've waited long enough. You guys hurry up. I've been wanting to come here for weeks. I'm not wasting another second."

"Come on, gang, let's go after him," said Joe. He grabbed Susannah by the hand and they both took off running. They finally caught up with him when they reached the carnival section of the park.

"Look at those covered wagons racing around that track over there," Danny exclaimed. "They're flying. I want to go on that right away."

"The line is a mile long," said Susannah. "It's a really popular ride. We may have to wait for over an hour."

Danny frowned. "I'm bummin'," he replied. "What about that one over there? The Squirt Gun Fight at the O.K. Corral? There are only about a dozen people in line."

"That's one of my favorites," Susannah told him.

"Oh, yeah," said Donnie, as he came up behind her. He took her by the arm and gently pulled her toward him. "Is it your *most* favorite?"

"Well," she began. Then she thought for a moment and shook her head no.

"What *is* your favorite attraction here?"

"Me!" Joe exclaimed, as he took hold of her other arm. "At least I hope so."

"No way," Donnie protested. "She's too smart for you. Aren't you, Susannah?"

Susannah didn't know what to say.

"I . . . ah . . . ," she stammered, her face turning red.

"Hey, Donnie, back off," Joe said angrily.

Donnie suddenly stepped back. "You know me; I was just foolin' around. I didn't mean any harm."

Joe felt bad that he had been harsh with his friend. He walked over and put his arm around Donnie's shoulder. "I'm sorry I snapped at you. It's just that I, well, I . . ."

Donnie interrupted him. "I know what you're trying to tell me." He leaned closer to Joe and said, "I'm sorry, too. I didn't realize how much you liked Susannah. I'll back off."

Joe reached around and gave Donnie a hug. "Thanks, man. I really appreciate it."

Chapter

5

JOE AND SUSANNAH TALKED TOGETHER while they waited in line with Biscuit and the other New Kids. When it came time for everyone to enter the Squirt Gun Fight arena, Danny leapt up and shouted, "All right! Which way do we go?"

The ride attendant was dressed in a bright blue cowboy shirt. The teenage boy handed each of them a belt with holsters and two squirt guns inside.

Danny swiftly strapped his around his waist. Then he reached down and pulled out both of the plastic guns at the same time. "Take that!" he said as he squirted Donnie in the face.

Donnie shook the water off. "Just you wait, Danny. You're going to be one soggy cowboy in no time at all."

The attendant left and quickly returned with an armload of white rain ponchos. He handed them out and instructed everybody to put them on.

Donnie took off his cowboy hat and slid his poncho over his head. "Hey, look, there's a giant bull's-eye on the front of this."

"There's another one on the back," said Jordan.

The ponchos had four giant rings painted on both the front and the back. The center ring had the number five inside. The second ring was marked with a four; the third, a three; and the fourth, a two. A number one was placed outside of the four rings.

"What's the deal with the bull's-eyes?" asked Danny.

"The object of this game," the attendant said, "is to shoot your squirt gun at the target on the other player's poncho. The ponchos are made of a special plastic that will turn blue when the water hits it. Each circle is worth a different number of points. The person who takes the fewest hits and ends up with the lowest score wins."

"I'm ready!" Danny declared. "Let's get rollin'."

"Is everyone else all set?" the attendant asked.

"I can't get this gun belt buckled," complained Jordan.

The attendant leaned over and took a closer look at it. "I think that one's broken. I'll go get you another one."

"I got news for you, big brother," said Jordan. "You'd better be careful because I'm going to be aiming right for you."

"You have to catch me first," Jonathan replied.

The attendant returned with a new belt and holster and gave it to Jordan.

He buckled it on easily. "I'm all set. Where do we go now?"

"Just step inside," said the attendant, swinging open a wooden gate. "You can go anywhere in the stables, the bunkhouse, the barn, or the corral. But be careful. There are booby traps everywhere!"

Danny was the first one through the

gate. Biscuit was right behind him. Donnie rushed around the bodyguard and ran up beside Danny.

"I'm going to wipe you out," said Donnie. "So beware!"

Danny laughed out loud. He raised his squirt guns high up in the air. "You'll never beat me!"

"You wanna bet?" asked Donnie.

"I'll bet you those new green tennis shoes that you won't."

"What?" cried Donnie. "Not my new shoes. I haven't even worn them yet."

"Exactly!" Danny replied. "You don't think I'd want them if you *had*. No way! I'd never wear an old pair of your shoes."

"What about my new belt?" suggested Donnie. "The one I got in New Mexico. I'll bet you that instead."

Danny shook his head. "No, you forgot that I bought one just like it. I want the shoes."

"How about my new video game?"

"No. I want the shoes."

"Would you take my toothpick collection?"

"No, only the shoes."

"All right," Donnie reluctantly agreed. "I'll bet you my new green shoes that I'll

win. But what about you? What do I get if
I win?"

"How about my new Celtics jacket al-
bum?" said Danny.

"It's a deal!"

Danny and Donnie shook hands. Then
they headed off toward opposite ends of
the stables. Jonathan and Jordan circled
around the outside of the barn, keeping a
close eye on each other every second.
Biscuit ducked down and hid behind
one of the large wooden horse troughs
that stood in the middle of the
corral. He waited and watched for the
others.

Joe and Susannah were so busy talking
they barely noticed that everyone else
had disappeared. They sat huddled together on a bench behind the bunkhouse.
Joe told Susannah about life with the
New Kids. He was happy that she under-
stood how hard they worked to put on a
good show.

"A lot of people don't understand," he
told her. "We like to kick back and relax,
but we don't get a chance to very often.
Today is our only day off this week."

"I'm glad that you had some time to
come to the festival," she said.

"And some time to spend with you," Joe replied.

Susannah started to blush. She didn't want Joe to see. She lowered her head so her curly red hair would cover her face.

Just as Susannah was about to ask Joe where he was planning to go on his vacation, they heard a loud crash!

She jumped to her feet. "What was that?"

She and Joe darted around the corner of the bunkhouse. They were surprised when they found Biscuit sprawled on his back in the horse trough. The water inside was pouring out over the edge. Biscuit was soaking wet.

Joe and Susannah both burst out laughing.

"What happened to you?" Joe asked.

"I found one of those booby traps."

"I think you lost the game," said Joe. "Your poncho has turned completely blue. There's not one speck of white left on it."

Biscuit struggled to get out of the trough. His arms were flying in every direction as he tried to find something to grab on to.

Joe reached out to help him but the bodyguard refused. Biscuit was stubborn. He was determined to do it himself if it was the last thing he did.

Joe tried not to laugh as Biscuit knocked the horse trough over on its side, but he couldn't stop himself. It was funny watching Biscuit flailing around on the ground.

Finally the bodyguard stumbled to his feet. He was dripping wet from head to toe.

"You'd better go back to the bus and change your clothes," suggested Joe.

Biscuit grumbled something under his breath but Joe couldn't quite hear it. He knew Biscuit was mad. Mad at himself.

Biscuit pulled off his poncho and his squirt gun belt. "I think you're right. I've got to get out of these wet things. But what about you guys? I can't leave the five of you here alone."

"Yes, you can," Joe replied. "No one will recognize us in these cowboy outfits. They haven't so far, have they?"

"No, I guess not. But you never know what could happen. Remember what Dick said about that rumor. I don't think

I should leave you. I'll call him and see if he can have someone bring me a change of clothes."

"I think I saw a phone booth right over there on Main Street," Joe told him. "You can call Dick from there."

"I'll go find it," said Biscuit. "I'll be back in a couple of minutes."

When the bodyguard left, Joe and Susannah went around behind the bunkhouse and sat down together again.

On the other side of the corral, Jonathan and Jordan were still stalking each other back and forth outside the barn. Jonathan had landed seven hits on his brother. Jordan had only been able to squirt Jonathan twice. He usually managed to dart away before the water could hit him.

Inside the stables, Danny and Donnie had climbed up into the hayloft and were furiously shooting it out. Danny's water was nearly gone, so he decided to make a direct attack. He climbed up on top of the bales of hay and dashed over to the other side of the loft. He leapt out at Donnie and pounded him with sprays of water.

Donnie aimed his squirt gun right at

Danny's poncho. He pulled the trigger and nothing happened. He squeezed it again and two drops dribbled out. He raised the other squirt gun and fired. Danny jumped to the right and the stream of water just missed him.

Donnie fired again. But this time the gun was dry. He tossed the empty pistol to Danny. "I'm all out of water," he declared.

Danny checked his water supply. He shook the guns upside down to see if there was a little bit left. His eyes lit up when he felt some inside. He gripped the guns tightly in each hand and he charged straight for Donnie. "Take that," he shouted as his last two shots landed right in the middle of Donnie's chest.

Donnie looked down to see how many times he had been hit. He counted all of the blue spots covering his poncho. When he looked up and saw that Danny had taken only three hits, he said, "It looks like you've won my green tennis shoes."

"I told you I would," Danny boasted.

"Wait until next time," Donnie replied. "I'll win them back."

"We'll see about that!" said Danny.

The two climbed out of the hayloft and headed out into the corral.

"Where is everybody?" asked Donnie. "I don't see them anywhere."

"Jonathan? Jordan?" Danny cried out. "Hey, Joe and Biscuit, where are you?"

All of a sudden they heard a loud noise. *Bam! Bam! Bam!*

"It's coming from over there," said Donnie, pointing toward the barn.

Danny and Donnie ran right over there, but they didn't see anyone.

Bam! Bam! Bam!

"Someone's inside that chicken coop," said Danny.

Donnie pulled open the door. Jonathan and Jordan shouted for joy.

"Yeah!" yelled Jordan. "You finally found us."

Donnie stepped into the little building. He laughed out loud when he saw the Knight brothers locked inside two large cages. "What are you doing in here?"

"We're scuba diving," Jonathan said sarcastically. "What does it look like?"

"Very funny," Donnie replied. "How did you get yourselves trapped in those cages?"

"If you step on that middle floorboard,

you'll find out," Jonathan grumbled. "Now let us out of here."

Donnie started to reach for the latch, then he stopped. "What'll you give me if I let you out?"

Jonathan raised his squirt gun. "I'll give you a squirt in the face."

"You can't fool me," said Donnie. "That thing is empty."

"Are you sure?" asked Jonathan.

Donnie nodded. "Yeah, look at Jordan. He's covered with blue. You couldn't have any water left."

"Maybe he doesn't," said Jordan. "But I do! Take that!" *Splash!* Three shots of water poured all over Donnie's face.

"Okay, all right, I give up. I'll set you free." He undid the latches and they all crawled out of the chicken coop.

"Have you guys seen Joe and Susannah?" Danny asked Jonathan. "And Biscuit, too?"

"No. I don't know where they are. I haven't seen them in a long time."

"Hey, Joe!" Danny shouted. "Where are you?"

"Over here," he yelled.

Joe and Susannah stepped out from behind the bunkhouse hand in hand.

When the other New Kids saw that their ponchos were still white, they all got mad.

"Hey, what have you guys been doing?" cried Donnie.

"There's not a mark on you," said Danny. "You haven't fired a shot."

"Sure we did," Joe replied, holding up his pistols and pulling the trigger. "Look. They're empty."

"Then how come there's not a blue spot on you?"

"We weren't aiming at each other," Joe explained. "We were aiming at that barrel over there beside the bunkhouse."

Danny looked at the streams of water on the ground leading up to the wooden barrel. "So who won?"

Joe pointed to Susannah. "She did. She put every single shot right inside."

"I'm not surprised," said Donnie. "So where's Biscuit?"

The others laughed when Joe explained what had happened to the bodyguard. Then they counted up the spots on each of their ponchos.

Donnie and Jordan were both covered with so many they didn't even bother to figure out their scores; they knew they had lost. But Danny and Jonathan only had a few spots apiece. They carefully counted each one.

"I have eight points," said Jonathan.

Danny added his up again. "I win. I have seven points. So what's my prize?"

"I've got it right here," announced the attendant as he walked up behind him. He handed Danny a bright yellow box with the park logo on top.

Danny pulled off the lid and looked inside. "What is it?" he asked.

"Let me see," said Donnie, grabbing the box. He pulled out a small metal object. "Hey, it's an armadillo. And look, it's got a key chain on it."

Danny inspected it more closely. He looked puzzled as he turned it over in his hand.

"The armadillo is the Laredo Village mascot," the attendant explained.

Donnie could tell that Danny didn't like his prize very much, so he said, "If you don't want it, I'll take it."

"What will you give me for it?" he asked.

"You already beat me out of my new green tennis shoes. I don't have much left."

"I'll give you a chance to win them both," said Danny. Then he turned to the attendant and asked, "What's the biggest challenge in the whole park?"

The boy thought for a second. "That's probably the Giant Cactus Climb competition. No, wait a minute. It's the Silver City Scavenger Hunt. That's right. That's definitely the biggest challenge. It's really hard."

"All right!" Danny cheered. "That sounds perfect. Are you up for the big scavenger hunt, Donnie?"

"Lead the way."

Chapter

6

SUSANNAH AND THE NEW KIDS quickly exited the Squirt Gun Fight arena. They went back to Main Street in search of Biscuit.

"I told him I thought there was a pay phone up here," said Joe. "But I must have been wrong. I don't see a phone anywhere."

"He probably went looking for one someplace else," said Jonathan.

"Maybe we should wait for him back at the Squirt Gun place," Jordan suggested.

"I don't want to sit around and waste

time," complained Danny. "This is our only day off. Let's head over to the scavenger hunt."

"But Biscuit will be worried about us," Jonathan replied.

"Don't sweat it, Jonathan," said Danny. "He'll understand why we left. He knows we don't get much free time. But if it will make you feel any better, we can give Dick a call and let him know what happened."

"I guess we can do that," Jonathan agreed reluctantly.

Danny pulled him by the arm into the crowd. "It'll be all right, you'll see."

"Where is the scavenger hunt?" Jordan asked.

"I'll show you," Susannah replied. "It's on the other side of Boot Hill."

"Have you ever been on the scavenger hunt?" asked Donnie.

"No, but I've always wanted to."

"Then this is your lucky day!" he told her as they all walked off together.

"I know," she said under her breath. Susannah still couldn't believe that she had actually met the New Kids. Her brother had told her all about each one. But she'd never dreamed that she would get the chance to meet them, much less spend the day with them.

"Turn down this way," she said, pointing to the left.

Joe edged up closer to her as they headed through the thick crowd of tourists.

"I think there are more people here now than when we first arrived," Jonathan commented.

"I like the way everyone is dressed up in western clothes," said Donnie. "Even the little kids. Sometimes I wish I had lived in the old West. I'd have been a gold miner or a brave Indian warrior. They would have called me Great Chief Soaring Eagle."

"I don't think so," Danny replied. "They probably would have named you Wimpy Little Chicken Heart."

Donnie made a face at Danny. "No matter what they called me, I'd have been strong and brave enough to beat you any day."

"Not a chance," Danny protested. "You could never outdo me."

"Just you wait," growled Donnie. "I'm going to blow you away in the scavenger hunt."

"*Ha!*" Danny roared.

"There's the booth up ahead," said Susannah.

"Let me at it!" Donnie exclaimed.

He rushed over to the little wooden building shaped like an old-West mining office. The sign overhead said SILVER CITY SCAVENGER HUNT in big block letters.

Donnie walked up to the ticket window and poked his head inside. "Hey, is anybody in here?"

A young girl in a cowboy hat stood up. "I am. What would you like?"

Donnie replied, "We want to go on the scavenger hunt."

"How many people do you have in your group?"

"Six."

"Do you want to go out alone or in groups of two or three?" the girl asked.

Joe leaned forward to answer. "In groups of two."

"Okay," she replied. "What level of difficulty do you want?"

"We'll take the hardest one you've got!"

"Are you sure about that?" she asked.

"Absolutely!" Donnie exclaimed.

"If that's what you want, that's what you'll get. But I guarantee, *it's hard!*"

"I'm not worried," he said, tipping down the brim of his red hat. "We can handle it."

"We'll soon find out," she replied.

Then the girl pulled three sheets of paper off the shelf and handed them to Donnie. "These are your lists of items to find. You can beg, borrow, or buy anything on here, but stealing isn't allowed. All the stuff on these lists is available somewhere in the park. If you get any of the items from outside the park, you'll be disqualified from winning the grand prize."

"What is the prize?" Donnie asked.

"It's a secret!" she answered.

"I don't care, anyway," he said. "I'm fighting for my name, my honor, and my new green shoes."

"Don't forget about the armadillo key ring," Danny added.

"Oh, yeah. That, too!"

"Who's going to team up with who?" asked Jordan.

"Susannah and I will be one team," Joe said, smiling at her.

Danny turned to Donnie. "Who's going to be your partner?"

"Not you, that's for sure."

"I'll be his partner," Jonathan offered.

Danny put his arm around Jordan. "It looks like it's you and me. Are you ready to blow them away?"

"I'd like nothing better than to beat that brother of mine."

"Here's your chance," Danny told him. "When do we start?"

"Let me give you these," said the girl.

She handed out three yellow backpacks with the Laredo Village logo on the flap. Inside each one was a Polaroid camera, loaded with film.

"What do we do with this?" asked Danny.

"You'll need the camera for one of the items on your list. And you can use the backpack to carry everything. The first pair that returns with every single item wins the grand prize."

"That'll be us!" Donnie proclaimed.

"Then you'd better get moving if you're going to make it back here before the park closes at ten o'clock."

"We have to be back long before that," said Jonathan. "We need to be finished by at least four-thirty, if not sooner."

The girl glanced at her watch. "It's

almost one o'clock. You'll never be able to finish by then."

"Oh, yes, we will," Donnie replied. "Just you wait and see."

He passed the other two teams their lists. There were seven items on each one, all of them different.

After reading through his, Donnie turned to the girl in the window. "You may be right after all. This could be real hard. I have to find a pitchfork, a raw egg, an old cowboy boot, a blue bonnet, the ace of diamonds, and . . . I don't understand the last two items. It says here I have to find something that starts with the letter *L*."

"That's correct," the girl replied. "You can bring back anything that starts with the letter *L*."

"Like what? Leprechauns or Lincoln Logs?"

The girl laughed. "Sure, if you can find either of those in the park, then they qualify."

"But what about this last one?" he asked. "It says here that I have to take our picture with a doctor, a nurse, or a buffalo."

"So what's your question?" said the girl.

"How do I do that?"

"You've got a camera in your backpack. Use it! Have you got any more silly questions?"

"No."

Danny held up his list. "I've got a question. It says here I have to take our picture with a grapefruit or a grizzly bear. Does that have to be a real grizzly bear? Or can it be a stuffed one or a picture of one or a statue of one or . . ."

The girl interrupted him. "Any kind is fine."

"The same is true for us?" asked Joe. "We have to get a picture with a monkey, a mayor, or a mule."

The girl nodded. "That's right. Any monkey, mayor, or mule will do."

Joe and Susannah read over their list. In addition to the photograph, they had to get a gold nugget, a red sock, a yellow flower, an arrow, something that started with the letter *H*, and a first-place blue ribbon from one of the carnival rides.

"We've already got two things on our list," Danny boasted.

Donnie pulled the paper away from

him. He read the items aloud: an orange feather, a horseshoe or harmonica, a cup of hot coffee, something that begins with the letter W, a photograph of a grapefruit or a grizzly bear, a first-place blue ribbon, and five different-colored bandannas.

Danny untied the red bandanna around his neck and Jordan handed him his blue one. "All we need is three more."

"I'm not giving you mine!" said Donnie. "You'll have to find your own."

"Come on, Jordan, let's get to it," Danny declared.

The three teams hurried off in three different directions, armed with maps of the festival grounds. Joe and Susannah set out toward the rodeo arena, hoping to find a red sock. Danny and Jordan went back to the main street in search of more bandannas. And Donnie and Jonathan went straight over to the Old West Ghost Town.

Chapter

7

DONNIE AND JONATHAN hurried through the carnival rides on their way over to the Old West Ghost Town. It was Donnie's idea to go there first. He wanted to check out the Buffalo Bill Café. He hoped to find a statue or sculpture of a buffalo that they could photograph.

The two singers climbed the hill up to the ghost town section of the park.

"This place sure is realistic," said Jonathan. "I love the way they made all of these buildings look old and beat up. It almost feels haunted."

"That's why they call it a *ghost town*," Donnie replied.

"Let's see if these *ghosts* have a pay phone somewhere. I want to call Dick about Biscuit as soon as possible."

Donnie glanced around. "I don't see one. But I'll keep on looking."

Donnie and Jonathan picked up speed when they spotted the café. They rushed across the sidewalk that ran in front of the restaurant and went inside. The place was full of tourists wearing western costumes, eating at small round tables.

Donnie looked everywhere in search of a buffalo. He didn't see one. There was nothing on the walls but old, torn wanted posters. Only a statue of Buffalo Bill stood in the corner. "I guess we're out of luck," he said sadly.

"Maybe not," Jonathan replied. "I bet we can get a raw egg here."

"You're right," Donnie exclaimed. "I almost forgot about that. Let's check out the menu." He pulled one off a nearby table and threw it open. After swiftly scanning the items, he shook his head. "No, they don't serve eggs here. Only hamburgers and hot dogs."

"Let's ask the waitress," suggested Jonathan. "They might have a few eggs in the kitchen anyway."

At that moment a teenage girl in a long old-fashioned dress came up to them. "Are you here to eat or are you looking for someone?"

"No," said Donnie. He turned his head to the side to make sure she couldn't see his face. "We're looking for a raw egg."

The waitress looked puzzled. "You want a *what*?"

"A raw egg," Donnie repeated. "Do you have one?"

"I don't know," she answered. "Why in the world do you want a raw egg? Are you on some kind of diet?"

"Well," Donnie began, "as a matter of fact, I have been changing my eating habits lately, but that's not why I want the egg. We're on a scavenger hunt and that's one of the items we have to find."

The waitress laughed. "Now I understand. I'll ask the cook if he has any eggs."

"Thanks a million," Donnie said. "We really appreciate it."

The teenage girl rushed off to the kitchen and Donnie and Jonathan waited by the cash register. When a young waiter carrying a huge tray of hamburgers walked past them, Donnie's eyes followed his every move as he set the plates down on a nearby table.

Jonathan noticed Donnie staring at the hamburgers. He could tell his friend was hungry, but he knew Donnie wouldn't eat unless he did. Even though he wasn't the least bit hungry, he said, "You know, Donnie, I'm starved. How about you?"

"I'll eat something if you do," he replied.

"Maybe we could get a couple of hamburgers to go," said Jonathan.

"Good idea. How many do you want?"

Jonathan didn't know what to tell him. He didn't want anything to eat. He had suggested they order hamburgers only to make certain Donnie did.

Just as he was about to answer, the waitress returned. "Do you have to get a *chicken* egg?"

"Why do you ask?" said Donnie.

"The cook has a couple of *duck* eggs in the refrigerator. Would one of those be okay?"

Jonathan pulled out the list of scavenger hunt items and read it carefully. "It doesn't say what kind of egg they want.

All it says here is that it has to be raw. I guess a duck egg will do just fine."

"Great," the waitress replied. "I'll go get one for you."

She started for the kitchen and Jonathan called out to her, "Wait a second. We'd like to order some hamburgers, too."

"How many?" she asked.

"Let's get two," answered Donnie.

"Two hamburgers coming right up!"

"No," Donnie said. "That's two hamburgers apiece!"

Jonathan was startled. He wasn't sure he could eat one, much less two. But he didn't complain. If that was what Donnie needed, he was determined to see that he got it.

It was only a few minutes before the waitress returned with the food. "I wrapped up the duck egg and put it inside a paper cup so it wouldn't get broken."

"We appreciate it," said Jonathan. "By the way, what are you doing with duck eggs?"

"The cook lives on a duck farm," she answered. "He brings them in and eats them for lunch."

73

"Are they good?" asked Donnie.

"Yeah. You should try them some-time."

"Maybe I will. Thanks again."

They paid their bill and rushed off to find an ace of diamonds.

Over on Main Street, Danny and Jordan quickly made their way to a souvenir shop.

When they went inside, Danny an-nounced, "We've come to the right place. Check out what I just found." He held up a bright yellow-and-white bandanna.

"Do they have more colors?" Jordan asked.

"Yeah. Tons of them. Let's take a green one and a brown one too. Now we have five different ones."

"And we found them in less than fif-teen minutes," said Jordan. "At this rate, we'll be done in no time at all."

Danny dug into his front pocket to get his money. Then he reached into his back pocket. "Oh, no. I'm not sure I have much money left."

"I'm not sure I do, either," Jordan re-plied.

"Wait a minute," said Danny. "I found

something." He pulled out a five-dollar bill. "This is all I have."

"Is five dollars enough to pay for those?" Jordan asked.

Danny checked the price tags. "They're a dollar and forty-nine cents apiece."

Jordan let out a sigh of relief. "Good, we've got just enough." They took the bandannas up to the checkout counter and gave the cashier the five-dollar bill.

As they waited for their change, Danny spotted a little boy wearing an Indian headband with an orange feather sticking up out of the back. "Let me see our list," he anxiously asked Jordan.

Jordan pulled it out of his pocket and Danny snatched it away.

"I thought so. It says here that we need an orange feather. That kid over there is wearing one."

Jordan looked around. "What kid?"

"He was right over there. I saw him, but now he's gone."

"Maybe he bought the feather here. Let's check it out."

The clerk handed Danny his change, and he and Jordan scurried through the shop in search of an Indian headband like the one the little boy had on.

"I don't think they sell them here," said Jordan. "I don't see any feathers any-where."

"Let's go find that kid and ask him where he got it. Or maybe we can talk him into letting us borrow it."

"Good idea," Jordan replied.

They both rushed out of the souvenir shop. The main street of Laredo Village was as busy as ever. Danny stood on his toes so he could see over the crowd.

"There he is," he shouted, pointing across to the other side.

The two singers dashed into the sea of tourists. They tried to get across the street as fast as possible, but there were so many people they could barely move an inch.

"He's getting away," cried Danny. "We've got to catch him before he disap-pears."

"But what can we do?" asked Jordan.

"I'm thinking, I'm thinking!" Then all of a sudden, his eyes lit up—he had come up with a plan. Danny reared back his head and pretended to sneeze. *Achoo! Achoo!*

Just as he was about to sneeze again, the people next to him stepped aside.

Achoo! Achoo!

They moved even farther away.

Jordan immediately caught on to Danny's plan and he pretended to sneeze, too.

The crowd slid away so fast Danny and Jordan were able to get to the other side of the street in no time at all. But when they arrived, the little boy with the orange feather was nowhere to be found.

Danny darted down the wooden plank sidewalk and rushed up to all the shop windows in turn. He looked in each one but he didn't see the boy. Jordan ran behind him and checked them out again. He didn't have any luck, either.

Danny stepped up onto a bench and scanned the crowd. "It looks like we lost him."

"No, wait!" cried Jordan. "There he is, over on the side street. I see an orange feather sticking out the window of that horse-drawn buggy. We'd better move fast. It's starting to pull away. Come on!"

Jordan took off running. Danny was right behind him. They ran out onto the side street, but the carriage was already a block away when they got there.

Danny spotted a second carriage and

rushed up to the driver. "Follow that buggy!" he yelled.

The teenage driver looked at him as if he were crazy.

Jordan grabbed Danny by the shoulder. "You can't take this buggy," he said. "We don't have enough money to pay for it."

"Oh, right. Cancel that order," he said to the driver.

Then he and Jordan tore off after the other carriage. It was speeding along faster and faster. Danny poured on a burst of power and shot ahead. Jordan raced to catch up.

"They're turning left," Danny cried. He sped around the corner and suddenly stopped in his tracks.

Jordan ran up beside him. "What's wrong? Why did you stop?"

Danny reached down to the ground and pulled up a small metal object. "Look. That horse just lost one of its shoes. It's just what we need."

"Nice going! But what about the orange feather?"

Danny looked around for the buggy. "There it is. It pulled up in front of that ride, the Texas Tumbler."

The two New Kids sped over to the carriage as fast as they could. When they got there, Danny leapt up onto the side step and looked inside. "He's gone!"

He jumped back down to the ground and yelled to the driver. "Where did your passenger go?"

The driver pointed up to one of the swirling metal cages on the Texas Tumbler.

"He's up there," Danny said to Jordan. Then he turned to the driver and asked, "How long does that ride take?"

The boy shrugged his shoulders. "It depends."

"It depends on what?" Danny asked.

"It depends on how many times you ride it."

Danny was starting to get frustrated. "Do you have any idea how many times he's going to ride?"

"Ten," the driver answered.

Danny slumped against the carriage. "That's great. We spent all this time chasing after him and now he's probably going to be up there for over an hour."

"We can't wait around that long," Jordan replied. "At least we found a horse-shoe. Let's go see what else we can find."

"We're on our way," said Danny.

Huge crowds of people were pouring into the rodeo arena when Joe and Susannah arrived.

"Have you ever been in a rodeo?" Susannah asked Joe.

"No. Have you?"

"Once," she answered. "When I was seven, I entered the pig-catching contest."

"Was it fun?"

"Sort of. I liked chasing the baby pig around the arena, but I was nervous doing it in front of so many people. I was afraid they'd laugh at me."

"I love crowds," Joe replied. "The more people the better. Ever since I was little, I've loved to get up onstage. I started doing plays at our neighborhood theater when I was six years old."

"I don't think I could ever do that," said Susannah. "I'd probably make a fool of myself."

"I bet you could do it if you really wanted to."

"Do you think so?"

"I'm sure of it."

"My best friend, Mona, asked me to try out for the school play with her. But I told her I was too scared to stand up in front of an audience. Maybe I should try out after all."

"That's the spirit!" Joe cheered. "Go for it. I just know you'll be great."

"I only hope I'm not terrible."

"You could never be terrible. You're too smart for that. Just make sure you memorize all of your lines and practice them until they feel natural, like they were your own words."

"Thanks," she said. "That sounds like a good idea. I'll do that."

"I'm glad to help. But I wonder where we should go now?"

"Why don't we head over to the rear entrance of the arena? That's where the performers get ready. I bet we'll find someone with a red sock back there."

They circled around the outside of the bleachers and Joe suddenly broke away and ran ahead.

"Hey, wait for me," yelled Susannah.

Joe stopped and bent down. He picked up something off the ground; then he rushed back to her. "Look what I found."

Susannah's eyes lit up. "A yellow flower. That's on our list."

Joe stepped closer to her and carefully placed the stem into the front pocket of her shirt. He then smiled and said, "You keep this safe."

"I will," she promised.

Joe turned and clapped his hands together. "I hope finding a red sock will be as easy as that was."

"I think you're about to get your wish," said Susannah. "Look over there."

Joe glanced around. "Where?"

"Under the bleachers."

Joe ran over to get a closer look. "I can't believe it. It's a red sock. This is amazing. We've already found two of our five items. This must be my lucky day."

"Mine, too," Susannah said, smiling to herself.

Joe placed the sock in their backpack. Then he put his arm around Susannah. "Now let's go see if we can find a monkey, a mayor, or a mule."

Chapter

8

DONNIE AND JONATHAN ran all over the ghost town in search of a deck of cards. First they tried the Trailblazer Gift Shop. When they went inside, the clerk told them that she had sold the last one ten minutes before.

The two singers were disappointed, but they pressed on. Next they went into a store that sold dollhouse miniatures, hoping that they might have a small set of cards. The woman behind the counter thought she had one somewhere, but she couldn't seem to locate it.

Donnie and Jonathan grew restless as

they watched her rummage through the storage cabinets. "I found a pair of miniature dice," she said. "Will those do?"

"No, we need a deck of cards," Donnie answered.

"I'm afraid I can't help you, then."

"Do you have any idea where we might find some?" asked Jonathan.

The woman thought for a moment. "There are quite a few souvenir stores here in the park. One of them may have a deck. Or else you could try the Lost Dutchman Diner. The employees play cards out back on their break."

"That sounds promising," Jonathan replied. "Where is this place?"

"Turn left at the sheriff's office up the street. It's two doors down."

"Thanks a lot," said Donnie.

They dashed out the door. He and Jonathan quickly made their way through the crowd and soon found the sheriff's office. They rounded the corner and raced over to the Lost Dutchman Diner.

"Let's go around to the back of the building," Jonathan suggested.

"There's an alley over here," Donnie

said, pointing to the right. "I bet it will take us there."

He and Jonathan scurried into the narrow passageway that ran between two old buildings. When they edged their way into it, they suddenly realized that the alley was getting smaller and smaller as they went along.

"It's becoming awfully tight in here," said Jonathan. "Do you think we can make it through to the other side?"

"Oh, sure," Donnie said confidently. "We can do it easily."

"I certainly hope so, because we can't go out the same way we came in. Look."

Donnie turned around. Then all of a sudden, he jumped back and let out a yelp. A big brown snake reared its head up in the air only two feet away. "Where did that come from? It wasn't there before."

"Well, it is now," said Jonathan. "Let's move on outta here."

Donnie rushed deeper into the alley. Jonathan was right behind him. They tried to press their way through to the other side, but the walls were even closer together.

The snake was sliding toward them, its head curled forward, ready to strike.

"We've got to squeeze through here somehow," said Jonathan.

"I'm trying, I'm trying," Donnie replied.

"Well, move faster. That thing is about to bite me."

"I can't go any faster. As a matter of fact, I can't go anywhere at all!"

"What? You have to!"

"No way. I'm stuck. I can't budge an inch."

Jonathan groaned. "Now what are we going to do?"

"It looks like the only way out of here is up. So here I go." Donnie reached over his head and grabbed onto one of the clapboards that ran up the side of the building. He took a deep breath and pulled with all his might until he rose up off the ground. "Follow me," he yelled to Jonathan.

"Follow you where?"

"I don't know. We'll find out when we get there."

"I guess I don't have much of a choice, so here goes." Jonathan pressed his back against the wall of the diner. He reached over to the other building and climbed his way up the side.

When the two singers were a safe distance away, they glanced back down at the snake below. The reptile was staring straight at them, its tongue slithering in and out.

"Come on," said Donnie. "We have to get to the roof. That's our only escape."

"Are you sure we can make it?" asked Jonathan.

"Absolutely," Donnie replied.

"I don't know about that. But I'll try."

The two of them used all their strength to move upward.

Jonathan was breathing harder and harder as he struggled to make the climb. "I'm not sure I can get there," he said.

"Yes, you can," Donnie told him. "Just concentrate."

Finally they managed to work their way up to the top. They were both exhausted when they pulled themselves onto the roof.

Jonathan leaned back and took off his cowboy hat. He wiped beads of sweat off his forehead and let out a sigh of relief.

"I told you we'd make it," said Donnie.

"You were right. Now where do we go?"

Donnie stood up and carefully walked along the roof to the back of the building.

"How are you doing down there?" he said to someone below.

Jonathan cautiously edged over next to him and peered over the edge. Three teenage girls were sitting around a picnic table.

"What are you doing up there?" asked one of the girls.

"We climbed up the side of the building so we could get a better view," Donnie replied.

"No, really," she said. "What's going on?"

Donnie told her about the snake and she jumped up out of her seat. "So that's where he went. I've been looking all over for him. I'm so glad that you found my pet snake. I've got to go catch him before he gets away again." The girl took off running.

"What is she doing with a snake?" asked Jonathan.

"Maria uses it in her act at the Death Valley Cabaret," said one of the other girls. "She keeps it in a cage in that trailer over there, but somehow it got loose. We've been looking all over for it. We'd almost given up hope of finding it."

At that moment, Maria returned with the long brown snake wrapped around her arm. "I found him," she said, holding him up for everyone to see. "He was sitting out front waiting for me."

"Is he all right?" the third girl asked.

"He certainly is. I think he's a little scared, though. You boys up there frightened him."

"*We* frightened *him?*" said Donnie. "I think you've got that backward. He scared us to death."

"I don't know why," Maria replied. "He's the nicest little snake I've ever met. He'd never hurt anyone."

"Do you mean he's *not* poisonous?" asked Jonathan.

"No way! I'd never use a dangerous animal in my act."

"I'd like to see this show of yours," Donnie said to her.

"I'm at the cabaret every night at eight o'clock. Come by sometime."

"I'll check it out," he answered. "But first we have to find some way to get down from here. Do you have any ideas?"

"Sure. Why don't you take the fire escape right below you?"

Donnie leaned over the edge of the building. He saw the black metal ladder running up the side. He and Jonathan climbed down it as quickly as they could.

"What's the fastest way around to the front?" asked Donnie.

"Wait," said Jonathan. "Don't forget why we're here."

"I completely forgot." Donnie then turned to Maria. "You girls wouldn't happen to have an ace of diamonds, would you?"

"A what?" she asked.

"An ace of diamonds," Donnie repeated.

The girls all looked at each other as if he were crazy.

"We're on the Silver City Scavenger Hunt," Jonathan explained. "We need to find an ace of diamonds. Someone told us that the employees here at the diner play cards on their break."

Maria nodded. "Now I get it. You need to see Don and Eddie. They're the cook and the dishwasher. They play cards all the time. I'll go get them."

Maria handed her snake to one of the other girls and hurried inside through the diner's back door. A few seconds later, two tall teenage boys returned with her.

"I see that you found your snake," said the blond one.

"These two guys found him. They're the ones who want to talk to you about a deck of cards."

Donnie told the boy what they needed. "I understand," he said. "There was some guy in the diner a couple of minutes ago who wanted one of the orange feathers out of the Indian headdress in the window."

"That was Danny and Jordan," Donnie replied. "We're trying to beat them."

"From the way they talked, they sounded like they're doing pretty well."

"Oh, no," cried Donnie. "We'd better get moving."

"Here's the card you're looking for."

The boy handed Jonathan the ace of diamonds. Jonathan thanked him; then he and Donnie said good-bye and rushed into the diner. They raced out the front door and down the street.

"Where to next?" asked Jonathan.

"Over there!" said Donnie. He pointed to a group of girls wearing long old-fashioned dresses and big sun hats. "The girl on the left is wearing a blue bonnet. That's just what we need."

Donnie bolted over to her. Jonathan followed right behind.

"Excuse me," Donnie said to the girl in the blue hat. "My friend and I are on a scavenger hunt and we need to locate a bonnet just like the one you're wearing."

"That's the worst line I've ever heard," she replied. "You should find a better way to meet girls."

"You don't understand," said Donnie. "I'm telling the truth. We really need a blue bonnet."

"It's true," Jonathan added.

"Really?" she asked.

"I swear," Donnie answered. "We're in a big hurry. Is there any way that we could beg, borrow, or buy your hat from you?"

"How much will you give me for it?"

Jonathan dug into his pocket to see

how much money he had. When he pulled out his hand, something fell to the ground.

The girl leaned down to get it for him. "What's this? It looks like a ticket." She turned it over and her eyes lit up. "It's a ticket to tonight's New Kids on the Block concert. You're lucky that you were able to get this. They were all sold out when I went to buy mine." She handed it back to Jonathan.

"We'll trade you the ticket for your blue hat," said Donnie.

"It's a deal." She untied the ribbon under her chin and handed it to Donnie.

He put it in the yellow backpack and zipped it up.

Jonathan gave her the ticket and she jumped for joy. She threw up her hands and shouted, "Hooray!"

"Now you can go with us to the concert," said one of the other girls.

"I'm so happy I got this ticket." She then reached over and gratefully hugged Jonathan. "Thank you."

When she pulled away, her arm accidentally bumped his black cowboy hat. He grabbed for it, but it was too late. It tumbled off and fell to the ground.

"It's Jonathan Knight!" the girls screamed at once.

"Look," one of them shouted. "And Donnie Wahlberg, too!"

"I want a souvenir," someone yelled.

"Uh-oh, we'd better get out of here," said Donnie.

He grabbed Jonathan by the arm and took off running. They sped through the crowd and raced across the street. Donnie ran up onto the wooden sidewalk in front of the general store. The girls charged after the two, screaming out their names.

"They're getting closer," cried Jonathan.

"I know how we can escape," said Donnie. "Follow me."

He hopped over the railing and out into the crowded street. Then he raced up to a horse and wagon parked in front of the old dance hall. He slipped around to the rear of the wagon and told Jonathan to climb inside. They lifted the heavy canvas covering and jumped underneath it.

Just as they pulled the canvas down tight, they heard the girls run past them.

"Jonathan, Donnie, where are you?" they shouted.

"I think I saw them over there," said one of the girls.

The two singers froze. They feared the fans had found them.

"Let's go look in the boardinghouse."

They were relieved when they heard the girls charge off down the street.

"Whew! That was close," said Donnie. "Let's get out of here."

Jonathan grabbed him by the arm. "No, wait! I think I hear something."

The two singers lay perfectly still. They listened carefully to every sound. Someone was walking around the wagon. They heard a rustling noise and, all of a sudden, the wagon started to move.

Donnie pushed at the canvas cover so he could climb out. "This thing won't budge. It's been tied down. We're stuck in here!"

Chapter

9

JOE AND SUSANNAH sat down on the grass together while they waited for the winner of the Hollering Contest to be announced. They talked and laughed about all of their favorite TV shows as the judges added up the scores of the six contestants.

"I bet you'll win," said Susannah. "I just know it."

"I'm not so sure about that," Joe replied. "I did lousy on that last yell."

"No way! You did great."

"We'll soon find out. I think they're about ready to tell us who won."

A teenage girl stepped up to the microphone. "The winner is Number Three."

"That's me!" Joe shouted.

"I knew you'd win," said Susannah.

Joe rushed up to the judge.

"Congratulations," she said. "You got the highest score this week." When she pinned the long blue ribbon on his shirt, she looked at him more closely.

Joe was afraid that she had recognized him. He lowered the brim of his cowboy hat so she couldn't see his face.

"I know you. You're Joe . . . ah . . . Joe . . ."

"No, that's not my name," Joe replied, hoping to throw her off the track.

"Yes it is. You're Joe Mc . . . Mc . . . McSweeny. We were in the fifth grade together. Remember?"

Joe was relieved. "Sorry. I'm not from around here."

"Really? I could have sworn that I recognized you."

"Don't worry about it. It happens to me all the time." He thanked her for the ribbon and hurried back to Susannah.

They left the Hollering Contest as fast as they could, before the girl could realize Joe's true identity.

"I'm getting hungry," said Joe. "How about you?"

"Yeah. I could use something to eat."

"Why don't we grab a couple of tacos from that lunch wagon over there?" Joe suggested.

"I'd love it."

They ordered their food and sat down at a picnic table.

"Maybe we should go to Kit Carson's Kiddie Rides next," said Susannah.

Joe took a quick drink from his can of soda. "Why do we want to go there?"

"I think we might have better luck finding a monkey or a mule there than we did at the stables."

Joe smiled at her. "Even though we didn't find anything, we had a lot of fun riding the horses, didn't we?"

"It was great," Susannah replied. "But we lost a lot of time. We're only half done with our list. I'm not sure we have much chance of winning."

"Yes we do. If we pour on the power, I know we can win!"

"Do you really think so?"

"Absolutely. Let's go!"

* * *

Danny and Jordan walked away from the Tumbleweed Toss competition, their heads hanging low.

"We lost again," said Jordan. "That's the second time in a row. I don't think we're ever going to win a blue ribbon."

As they slowly walked through the crowd, Danny replied, "We'll find something we can win."

"Maybe we should try and locate an object that begins with a *W* first."

"Like what?"

Jordan shrugged his shoulders. "I don't know. How about a worm or a wig? Or maybe a woodchuck or a wallet."

"A whistle!" said Danny.

"Where are we going to get one?" asked Jordan.

"I don't know."

Danny and Jordan sat down on a near-by bench. They were both discouraged. Danny kicked at the ground with his shoe. Jordan leaned his head back and closed his eyes. Neither said a word.

Danny absentmindedly stared into space until all of a sudden he spotted Joe and Susannah off in the distance. They were running side by side. He watched them disappear behind the Billy-the-Kid Bumper Cars.

Then all of a sudden, Danny leapt to his feet. "This is no way to act," he cried. "We can win this contest, but we have got to get serious."

He pulled out his park map and searched through the listings. "There must be a competition where we can win a blue ribbon."

Jordan stretched out his arms. "Are there any singing or dancing contests?"

"Nope. But there's an Apache Triathlon. You have to throw a tomahawk, put up a tepee, and build a campfire. Or maybe this would be good. The Santa Fe Lizard Races. No! I like the sound of this—the Rocky Mountain Maze."

Jordan pulled the map out of his hand. "Let me take a look at that." He read it over, then said, "I think we should try the Texas Chili Chowdown. I bet we could win a blue ribbon there. Besides, I'm getting hungry."

"Me, too," Danny agreed. "Let's go wolf down some chili."

"It's not far from here. It's just around the corner."

Danny and Jordan took off. They sped straight there. They arrived just as the attendant was asking if anyone else wanted to enter the competition.

"We do!" They both shouted at once.

"Come on up here and take a seat," said the young man.

He pointed to the long wooden table where five people were all ready to begin. Danny and Jordan slid into their chairs. A girl ran over and wrapped big white aprons around them and tied their hands behind their backs. "You'll have to take off your cowboy hats," she said. "You won't be able to eat the chili very well if you leave them on."

Danny and Jordan looked at each other. They weren't sure what they should do. They knew if they took off their hats, someone might recognize them. But if they didn't, they'd lose the competition.

"What the heck," said Danny. "Let's do it."

She removed their hats and put them on a shelf.

"It looks like we're all set," said the man. "Bring on the chili!"

The girl wheeled out a cart full of huge

white bowls. She put one down in front of each contestant.

"Let's win this one!" said Jordan.

"We will!" Danny replied.

At that moment, the man held up a starter gun. "On the count of three, dive in! The one who eats the most in the next sixty seconds will be our big winner.

"One, two, three."

Bang!

Danny smashed his face down into the chili. He gobbled it up as fast as he could. Tomato sauce and kidney beans were smeared all over him.

Jordan tried something different. He put his cheek down on the edge of the bowl and tipped it sideways. The chili poured straight into his mouth. He swallowed it up in record time.

"There's only ten seconds left," the man yelled. "Hurry up!"

Danny bobbed his face in and out of the brown gooey mess so fast he spattered chili into his hair and down his neck.

Jordan tipped the bowl even farther so he could get a few more gulps before time ran out. He leaned it over even farther and it started to wobble. He tried to stop it, but the bowl flipped around and landed on top of his head. Chili poured all over his face.

"Time's up!" the man shouted. "Let's see who won."

He laughed when he saw Jordan sitting there with a bowl on his head. "You didn't win," he said to him. "But let's see who did."

The girl rushed over to Jordan and pulled the bowl off. She untied his hands and handed him a wet towel.

The man measured everyone's chili with a ruler. "We have a winner down here," he said, holding up a woman's arm.

Danny and Jordan leaned over to see who it was. They were surprised to discover a tiny white-haired woman beaming victoriously.

The man handed her a blue ribbon. "You won again, Agnes. No one can beat you."

Danny and Jordan couldn't believe they had lost to a little old lady half their size. They weren't happy they had lost, but they were determined to press on.

They cleaned themselves up and reached for their cowboy hats.

Just as they were about to put them on,

the girl walked over to them. "Could I . . . could I . . . have your autograph?" She nervously held out a piece of paper.

Jordan smiled at her. "Of course. We'd be glad to."

The girl watched his every move as he wrote down his name. She kept right on staring even after he passed it to Danny.

When Danny was finished, he tapped her on the shoulder. She looked up into his eyes and nearly fainted. "It's really you. Danny and Jordan. I can't believe it. Wow."

"Would you do us a favor?" Danny asked.

"Anything. What is it?"

"Please don't tell anyone you saw us. At least not until later. We don't want to be mobbed."

"Oh, I won't tell a single person, I promise."

"Thanks," said Jordan. He then leaned over and kissed her on the cheek.

Danny kissed her, too, and they waved good-bye.

The girl watched them until they disappeared into the crowd.

Chapter

10

OVER ON THE OTHER SIDE of the park, Donnie and Jonathan were still trapped inside the wagon.

"I think we've stopped," said Jonathan. "Maybe we can finally get out of here."

"Be quiet," Donnie whispered. "Someone's coming around to the back."

The two singers heard people talking but they couldn't make out what was being said. They noticed the rustling sound again and then everything was silent.

Donnie couldn't wait another second. He pushed at the canvas. It started to rise up. "They untied it. Now we'll be able to get out. Come on, let's go."

"Be careful," Jonathan warned. "Check to see who's out there."

Donnie lifted the edges of the canvas and peered out. "I don't see anyone."

"Can you tell where we are?"

"It looks like some kind of barn or stable."

Donnie threw back the cloth cover and began to climb over the side.

"Wait," said Jonathan. "Don't forget your cowboy hat." He handed it to Donnie. Then he looked around for his own. "What happened to my hat? Oh, now I remember. I dropped it back at the ghost town. What am I going to do now?"

Donnie reached into the yellow backpack. He pulled out the blue bonnet and tossed it to him. "Wear that!"

"What!? Are you crazy? Do you expect me to walk around with this silly thing on my head?"

"What else have you got to wear?"

Jonathan sighed. "Nothing, I guess."

He reluctantly picked up the bonnet and tried it on.

"I think it goes the other way," said Donnie.

Jonathan turned the hat around. He tied the ribbon under his chin. "Come on, Donnie, let's get out of here. We've still got a lot of things to find if we're going to win this scavenger hunt."

"Don't worry," Donnie replied. "We're going to win. The first thing we have to do is figure out where we are."

They both jumped out of the wagon. Rows of horse stalls ran in both directions. Straw covered the ground.

"I don't see a door or a window anywhere," said Jonathan. "What is this place?"

"Beats me. Let's go down this way. Maybe we'll find out."

Donnie led Jonathan off to the right, past more rows of stalls. They turned the corner and hit a dead end. When they started back the way they came, they suddenly heard someone whistling.

"What should we do now?" asked Jonathan.

"Maybe they'll be able to tell us where we are," said Donnie.

"But what if we're not supposed to be in here?"

"We're not doing anything wrong. We won't get in trouble."

Just then a tall, muscular man came around the corner. "Hey, what are you two doing back here? This is a restricted area. No tourists allowed."

"Well . . . ah . . . we got lost," said Donnie.

The man walked over to them. He stared Donnie in the eye. "You're that little punk who stole my saddle!"

"No, not me. I just got into town this morning."

"Do you expect me to believe that story?"

"It's true," said Jonathan.

"We're going to find out what's true, all right." The man reached out and grabbed Donnie by the arm. "I'm taking you down to police headquarters, where we'll straighten this out."

Donnie tried to break free, but the man held on tight. "I didn't take your saddle! I'm telling you the truth."

The man laughed. Then he jerked Donnie forward. "I don't like your attitude. I think I'll show you what happens when you steal from me!"

The man reared back his fist and swung at him. Donnie leapt to the side. Jonathan shoved the man in the back and he fell forward. Donnie pulled away and they both took off running. They darted down a row of stalls and turned to the left.

They spotted a large, open doorway up ahead. But just as they were about to run for it, they heard someone coming. They ducked into one of the stalls. Donnie found a pitchfork sticking out of the hay. He lifted it up and held it out, ready to defend himself.

"I don't hear anyone now," said Jonathan. "Let's make a break for the exit."

The two edged their way out of the stall. The coast was clear. They ran for the doorway. They didn't look back.

"We're almost out of here," said Donnie, waving the pitchfork over his head. "It's just a few more feet."

The two singers burst through the exit. They were shocked to discover that they had run out into the middle of the rodeo arena.

The crowd clapped and shouted when they appeared.

Donnie and Jonathan didn't know what was going on. But they soon found out.

The announcer on the loudspeaker said, "And our next act is the Diddle Brothers, the best rodeo clowns west of Fresno!"

The crowd cheered again. Donnie and Jonathan waved back to them.

"What do we do now?" asked Jonathan, as he tightened the ribbon on his bonnet.

"Sing a few bars of 'Hangin' Tough'?"

"I don't think that's what these people are waiting for."

"Then what do you suggest?"

"I suggest we get away from that bull over there."

Donnie swung around. A huge black bull was charging across the arena, heading straight for them.

He and Jonathan were so surprised they both leapt into the air and almost fell over backward. The crowd burst out laughing. Donnie shook the pitchfork at the bull and Jonathan pulled the red bandanna off his neck and waved it out in front of him as the bull rushed toward them.

The crowd laughed again.

When the giant creature came closer, Donnie and Jonathan ran in opposite directions and circled behind it. The animal chased after them again.

All three ran back and forth around the arena. Each time Donnie and Jonathan fell down, the audience roared with delight. The crowd never suspected it wasn't part of the show. They loved every minute of it. But Donnie and Jonathan were getting tired. They wanted to get out of there.

Fortunately, at that moment a man on horseback rode up to them. He was swinging a lariat over his head. He circled around the bull three times, then threw the rope across its shoulders. He jumped out of his saddle and wrestled it to the ground.

The audience leapt to its feet and screamed, "Hooray!"

Donnie and Jonathan saw their

chance to escape. They raced over to the front entrance and leapt over the gate. As they ran into the park, they could hear the announcer say, "Let's give a big hand to the Diddle Brothers!"

At the same time as Donnie and Jonathan were setting out in search of a cowboy boot, Joe and Susannah were rushing over to the Winchester Gold Mine.

"Do they really have gold there?" Joe asked.

"Yeah. The dirt has tiny little flakes of gold sprinkled through it. You swish it around in a pan of water. The dirt washes away and the gold flakes fall to the bottom."

"But we have to get a gold nugget," said Joe. "Is a little flake of gold good enough?"

"I don't know. I didn't think of that. Maybe we shouldn't go to the gold mine after all."

"But where else can we get a gold nugget?"

Susannah stopped. She thought for a moment. "The only place I can think of is Sutter's Mill Jewelry Store. They have little gold nuggets made into earrings, necklaces, and tie tacks."

"That sounds great," said Joe. "Let's go there instead."

He and Susannah turned around and headed back through Main Street. They quickly found the jewelry store and went inside.

Susannah rushed up to the display counter. She pointed to a row of chains with tiny golden nuggets hanging from them. "There they are. Aren't they pretty?"

"May I help you?" said the clerk.

"Yes," Joe replied. "I'd like to look at those necklaces."

The clerk lifted out the tray. Joe carefully examined them all. He lifted one out and showed it to Susannah. "How do you like it?"

"It's beautiful."

"It's yours," he said. He lifted it over her head and placed it around her neck.

"But . . . but you shouldn't get this for me. It's too expensive."

"No, as a matter of fact, it doesn't cost very much at all. I hope you don't mind.

I just wanted you to have a souvenir of today."

Tears started to well up in Susannah's eyes. She threw her arms around Joe. "Thank you. I'll wear it forever."

Chapter

11

DANNY AND JORDAN were excited when they finally tracked down a grizzly bear to photograph. They had searched everywhere. They found it in the Mt. McKinley Juice Bar. The giant bear statue loomed out over the room.

Danny and Jordan both wanted to be in the picture, so they talked the waitress into taking the shot.

When she handed it to them, Danny broke into a big smile. "It's perfect!"

Jordan was happy, too.

"Thanks a lot," he said, shaking her hand.

"Come back anytime," she replied.

"I just might do that," Jordan told her as they headed for the door.

The minute they got outside, Biscuit grabbed them both by the arm. "I found you!"

"Hey, Biscuit, where have you been?" asked Danny. "We looked all over for you, but we couldn't find you anywhere."

"When I went to call Dick, a crowd of girls recognized me and chased me across the park. I finally got away from them and went back to the bus to change my clothes."

"Those are pretty slick ones you've got on," said Jordan. "You look like a real cowboy in that flannel shirt and ten-gallon hat."

"Those cowboy hats worked for you guys. I figured one would do the same for me. So where are the other New Kids? They didn't get into trouble, did they?"

"I don't know," answered Danny. "We haven't seen them in a long time."

"What!?" cried Biscuit. "Why not?"

Danny explained about the scavenger hunt. Then he told the bodyguard that they didn't have time to talk. They had to hurry away to find a blue ribbon.

"Oh, no. You're not going anywhere," he said. "Dick gave me strict orders to round up you guys and take you back to the theater."

"How come?" asked Jordan. "Dick said we could stay here until it was time for the show."

"I know. But Dick heard on the radio about some girl who claims to have spotted Jonathan! Now hundreds of girls are running all over the park, looking for the New Kids."

Danny and Jonathan tipped their hats down a little lower. "We'll be *extra* careful."

"No. Dick says I have to bring you back."

"But we don't want to go," said Jordan. "We want to finish the scavenger hunt."

"Sorry. There's nothing I can do about it."

Danny let out a sigh. He didn't want to leave any more than Jordan did. But he didn't see any way out of it. Then all of a sudden, he got an idea.

He slowly circled around behind Biscuit. He signaled to Jordan that he had a plan. Then he reached up and grabbed both sides of the bodyguard's ten-gallon hat and pulled it down as hard as he could.

"Let's go!" he shouted to Jordan as Biscuit, taken totally by surprise, struggled to pull the hat off his face. Before he was able to, they took off running. They dashed through the streets at top speed, weaving in and out of the tourists. They turned left and raced between two buildings. Then they headed back to the carnival rides.

Danny pointed to the North Woods Log-rolling competition. "I bet we can win this one with our fancy footwork."

"You're right. Why didn't we think of that before?"

"Beats me. Let's just go inside and show them what we can do. Blue ribbon, here we come."

The next round of competition was about to begin. Danny and Jordan lined up on their logs right next to three other competitors.

A teenage girl held up a starting gun. "When I pull the trigger, the logs will begin rolling. We won't stop until there's only one person left. Let me remind you, the longer you stay on, the faster the logs will roll. Is everybody ready?"

"Yes," they all answered.

Bang! She fired the gun.

The logs started to turn slowly at first, but they quickly speeded up. They rolled around in a shallow pool of water, making them wet and slippery and hard to stand up on.

Danny struggled to keep his balance at first, but he soon got the hang of it. So did Jordan.

Within seconds, the first contestant dropped out. He stumbled into the water and staggered over to the sidelines.

Two more people fell. Then Danny and Jordan were the only ones left.

"We won!" Danny yelled.

"But which of us gets the blue ribbon?" asked Jordan.

"What difference does it make? We've got it."

"It makes a difference to me!" said Jordan.

"All right, then we'll fight to the finish."

The two singers pumped their legs up and down as fast as they could. The attendant raised the speed and they pumped even harder. She turned it up again and they used all their strength to keep their balance.

Finally, she pushed the speed dial as high as it would go. The logs flew around so fast Jordan started to wobble.

Danny laughed when he saw Jordan weaving back and forth. "I'm going to win," he boasted. Then all of a sudden he flew forward and splashed into the water.

"Ha!" cheered Jordan. "You lose!"

The attendant rushed over and gave Jordan his blue ribbon. "I've never seen anything like that. No one's ever gone that fast. How did you do that?"

"Just lucky, I guess."

"That was amazing. You must be some kind of Olympic athlete or something."

"No," said Jordan. "We're just a couple of tourists."

"No, you're not. You're Jordan Knight! I don't believe it. Hey, Carolyn, come here. It's Jordan. And look, it's Danny, too!"

A dark-haired girl ran out. She jumped up and down, screaming, "Danny! Jordan!"

The New Kids turned and tore off in

the opposite direction. The girls were right behind them, shouting their names at the top of their lungs. Everyone turned to see what was going on. When other young girls realized that it was Danny and Jordan, they joined in the chase. They pursued them through the carnival rides and over to Main Street. More people joined in every step of the way.

Danny and Jordan tried to escape by ducking into the riding stables, but girls soon caught up with them.

"Is that Donnie over there?" asked Jordan. He pointed into the corral as they circled around it.

Danny turned to look. "That's him on top of that buffalo. Hey, *Donnie!*" he shouted. *"Help!"*

Donnie jumped down from the buffalo. "Did you get the picture?" he yelled to Jonathan.

"Yeah. It came out perfect."

"Now let's kick it outta here and rescue Danny and Jordan. I've got a great idea about how we can do it. Follow me."

Donnie grabbed up his pitchfork and raced off. Jonathan held on to his blue bonnet as he and Donnie ran up behind the fans.

Donnie spotted the Rocky Mountain Maze up ahead and flew up to the entrance. He pulled his red hat down over his eyes and yelled as loud as he could. "Hey, everybody. The New Kids went in here!"

The crowd immediately turned around and charged over to the maze. They poured inside.

Donnie and Jonathan slapped their hands together as the last one disappeared into the ride.

"Nice job!" said Jonathan.

"I have to admit it, my plan worked out pretty well. Now let's see if we can make it back to the scavenger hunt booth before the others."

Danny and Jordan stopped to catch their breath at the Buttes and Valleys Roller Coaster.

"It looks like the coast is clear," said Jordan.

"What a relief," Danny replied. "Now all we have to do is get a cup of hot coffee and we have everything on our list."

Jordan pointed to a trailer decorated like a wagon. "There's a chuck wagon over there. Maybe they sell coffee."

The two singers rushed to the window and asked for a cup of coffee.

The girl inside handed him a small paper cup. "That will be one dollar."

"Oh, no," said Danny, digging into his pocket. "I've got less than fifty cents."

"I'm sorry," said the girl, pulling the cup away. "It costs a dollar."

Danny checked his pockets again. Then he searched through the backpack.

"Would you trade me this for the coffee?" He placed the armadillo key chain down on the counter.

The girl picked it up. "Sure, why not? I've been wanting to get one of these for my boyfriend." She handed him back the coffee.

"You'll never know how much I appreciate this," Danny told her. "I can't thank you enough."

Danny gripped the cup tightly in his hand. "Now our list is complete. If we hurry, we might be the first ones back."

He and Jordan took off at top speed. They dodged in and out of the crowd and up and down the sidewalks. They raced around Boot Hill and headed for the Silver City Scavenger Hunt.

"We're almost there," cried Danny.

"And so are they," shouted Jordan. "Here come Donnie and Jonathan."

Danny pointed to the left. "And Joe and Susannah, too."

Jordan started to run even faster. "We've got to get there first!"

Everyone ran straight for the front window. The same girl was still working inside. She jumped back when she saw them charging at her.

A split second later, all three teams stormed up to the window at the same time.

"We won!" cried Donnie.

"No, we did!" yelled Danny.

"You're both wrong," said Joe. "We got here first."

They all started to shout at once. "No way! You're crazy! We're the winners!"

"Whoa. Slow down," said the girl in the window. "I won't know who won until I check off all the items on your lists. So who's going to go first?"

"We are," Donnie replied. He leaned the pitchfork up against the side of the building. Jonathan took off his blue bonnet and set it down on the counter.

"What are you laughing at?" he asked Jordan.

126

"You don't know? I've never seen you look sillier than you did in that hat."

Jonathan made a face and turned away.

Then Donnie emptied out everything in the yellow backpack.

The girl looked the items over. She picked something up and asked, "What's this?"

"Lint," Donnie answered. "It starts with the letter *L*, doesn't it?"

"That's right," she replied. "It qualifies."

Donnie beamed proudly.

She carefully went through the other things and checked them off on her clipboard. When she was done, she said, "Congratulations. You found everything."

"All right," Donnie cheered.

"We're next," said Danny. He set down the cup of coffee and dumped out his backpack.

"Where's your item that starts with a *W*?" the girl asked.

"Oh, I almost forgot." Danny reached into his shirt pocket and pulled out a handful of green leaves. "This is ragweed."

"That starts with *R*," said Donnie. "You lose!"

"No, wait a minute." The girl looked more closely at the leaves. "This is a tricky one," she said. "It is ragweed. But it's also just a plain weed. So I'll accept it. It looks like you've completed your list, too!"

Danny shook his fist in the air. "We did it!"

Next Joe placed all of his and Susannah's items on the counter.

The girl picked up their photograph. "You got a picture of Mr. Wolinski, the mayor of Red Rock."

"That's right," said Joe. "We saw him with his family over by the blacksmith shop."

"That was clever," the girl replied. "Nice going."

She checked off their other items, including the gold necklace and a dozen strands of Joe's hair. "It looks like all three teams found everything on their lists. I'm amazed that you did it so fast."

"So who wins?" asked Jonathan.

She thought for a moment. "It looks like you all do."

"But what about the grand prize?" asked Danny. "Who gets it?"

"And what about my green shoes?" cried Donnie. "What's going to happen to them?"

"I'll give them back to you," Danny replied. "It's the least I can do for you after the way you helped us escape from those fans."

Donnie put his arm around Danny. "Thanks a lot, old pal."

The girl held out three yellow envelopes. "You *all* get prizes."

Donnie grabbed an envelope and tore it open. His face fell when he saw what was inside.

"What's the matter?" asked Jonathan.

Donnie showed everyone two tickets to the New Kids concert.

Jonathan shook his head in amazement. "I don't believe it."

The others opened their envelopes. They also received tickets.

"How come you're so unhappy about the concert tickets?" asked the girl. "Don't you like the New Kids?"

"We love them!" said Donnie. "It's just that, ah . . . well . . ."

Before he could finish what he was going to say, Biscuit ran up to them.

"There you are," he said. "Now I've got you. You guys are coming with me right away. You've got a show to do in less than half an hour."

"We're ready to go," Jonathan replied. "But what about all these things we collected? What should we do with them?"

The girl suddenly realized who he was. "You're Jonathan Knight." She looked at the others. "You're the New Kids on the Block. I don't believe it!"

"It's true," said Jonathan. "I'm afraid we're going to be late for our next concert if we don't hurry. What should we do with all of this stuff?"

"You can have it, or I'll take care of it."

Joe reached over and picked up the gold nugget necklace and put it back on Susannah. Then he grabbed the yellow flower and said, "I'm all set to go."

Danny picked up the picture of the grizzly bear. Jordan took his blue ribbon.

The girl held out the blue bonnet to Jonathan. "Do you want this?"

"No, you can keep it as a souvenir!"

Donnie grabbed the photo of himself on the back of the buffalo. Then he gave the girl his concert tickets. "These are for you."

The others handed over theirs, too.

"Thanks a lot!" she said. "I get off work in a couple of minutes. I'll call all my friends and go right over to the theater."

"We'll be looking for you," said Donnie.

"Let's move," shouted Biscuit. "Or there won't be a concert."

Chapter

12

EVERYBODY RAN BACK to the front entrance of the park and climbed onto the tour bus. The New Kids hurried to the back to change their clothes. Everyone except Donnie. He slumped into one of the seats up front.

Jonathan noticed that he looked pale and tired. He rushed over to Biscuit and whispered in his ear.

The bodyguard quickly dug into the refrigerator and pulled out a huge tray of food. He set it down next to Donnie and told him, "Be sure to eat something before show time."

Jonathan walked up beside Donnie

and placed his hand on his shoulder. "Please, Donnie, you've got to start eating more food. You're hurting yourself because you're not eating enough. I hate to see you this way. It really upsets me."

"But what about last night? It was my fault that your shoe was ruined. If I didn't eat so much, it wouldn't have happened."

"It wasn't the food that was the problem," said Jonathan. "It was your attitude. But now that you understand that, you won't hurt me or anyone else just because you want something to eat. Right?"

"That's true. I'll never do it again." Donnie let out a sigh of relief. "Now I can have a *real* meal. I thought I was going to starve today."

Donnie dug into the plate of food and wolfed it down in no time at all. He changed into his concert clothes just as they arrived at the theater.

Dick Scott ran out to the bus when they pulled to a stop. "You've got two minutes to get out onstage."

"We'll be there!" said Jonathan as he ran for the stage door.

Everyone else followed him. Joe waved good-bye to Susannah and Biscuit took her to her seat. She sat in the front row, anxiously waiting for the show to begin.

Finally the stage lights began flashing. Music poured out across the theater. The New Kids burst onto the stage and the crowd went wild.

The fans cheered even louder when they started to sing "Step by Step."

Susannah was overjoyed when they broke into their second song and Joe pulled her up onstage. He gently held her by the hand as he sang:

"Please don't go, girl.
You would ruin my whole world.
Tell me you'll stay.
Never, ever go away."

BACKSTAGE SURPRISE

BLOCK PARTY

WORKIN' OUT

ON TOUR

ON STAGE

BETWEEN BROTHERS

(On-Sale August 15, 1991)

WHERE'S JOE?

(On-Sale October 15, 1991)

ARCHWAY PAPERBACKS
PUBLISHED BY POCKET BOOKS